Wind Power

by Tracy Vonder Brink

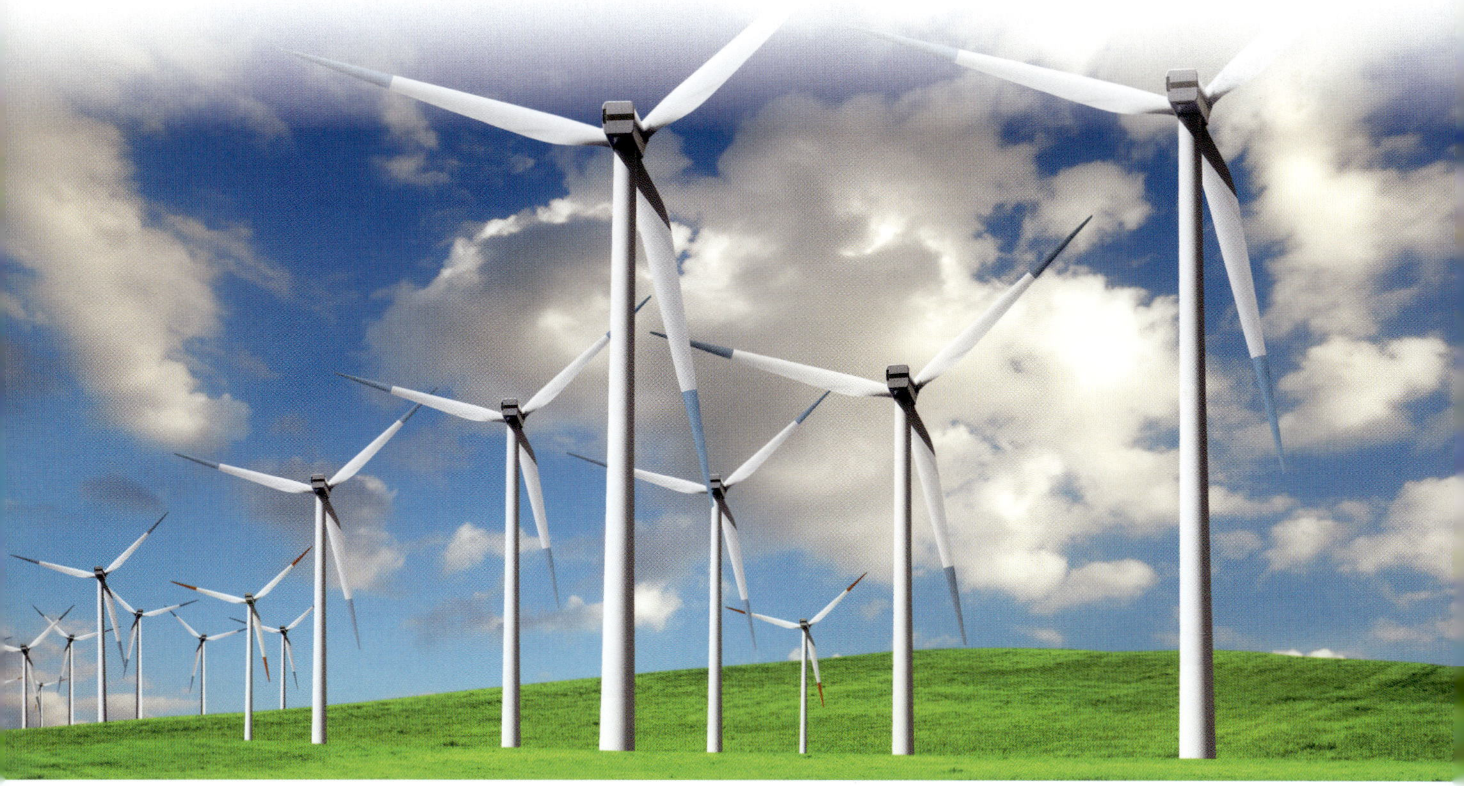

A Crabtree Crown Book

School-to-Home Support for Caregivers and Teachers

This appealing book is designed to teach students about core subject areas. Students will build upon what they already know about the subject, and engage in topics that they want to learn more about. Here are a few guiding questions to help readers build their comprehension skills. Possible answers appear here in red.

Before Reading:

What do I know about wind power?

- *I know wind can be strong.*
- *I know I cannot see the wind.*

What do I want to learn about this topic?

- *I want to know how wind power makes electricity.*
- *I want to learn how wind farms work.*

During Reading:

I'm curious to know...

- *I'm curious to know how electricity from a wind farm goes to a building.*
- *I'm curious to know the name of the largest wind farm in the United States.*

How is this like something I already know?

- *I know buildings have electricity.*
- *I know the United States has wind farms.*

After Reading:

What was the author trying to teach me?

- *The author was trying to teach me what wind power is.*
- *The author was trying to teach me how wind power can replace fossil fuels.*

How did the photographs and captions help me understand more?

- *The photographs helped me understand how wind farms work.*
- *The captions gave me extra information.*

Table of Contents

Chapter 1: Energy and Fuel

We need energy for everything we do. Energy heats our homes. Our bodies use it to live. It fuels our cars. But what is energy?

In science, work is energy moving from one object to another. Your feet pushing against your bike's pedals are doing work that makes the bike move.

Energy is the ability to do work or to make something happen. Energy is everywhere. It comes in different forms. Heat, light, and sound are all forms of energy. The battery in your phone uses electrical energy.

Transforming Energy

Energy can be transformed, or changed, from one form to another. Energy changes forms when it is used to make something happen. Wood has energy locked inside it. Burning the wood changes its energy into heat and light.

Heat and light are two forms of energy.

A fuel is something that is changed in some way to produce energy. Wood is a fuel because burning it releases heat and light. Food is fuel for your body. Your body breaks down what you eat and uses it as energy.

Fossil Fuels

Fossil fuels are nonrenewable energy sources. Nonrenewable means they cannot be replaced.

We use fuels to make heat and power. Coal, oil, and natural gas are fuels. They are burned to release their energy. They all come from underneath the ground and they formed over millions of years. These types of fuels are called fossil fuels. If we use them up, they cannot be replaced.

Climate Change

Fossil fuels give off **carbon dioxide** when they are burned. Carbon dioxide collects in a layer around Earth. This layer traps heat and warms the planet. As Earth becomes warmer, its **climate** changes. We need energy sources that will not run out and that will not change the climate. We need **alternative** sources of energy. One such source is wind power.

Climate change harms people and animals. Impacts of climate change include higher temperatures and changes in rainfall. This can lead to wildfires and less water for crops. These changes affect where people and animals live and the food that they eat.

Chapter 2: What Is Wind?

The air that surrounds all of Earth is called the atmosphere. Air pressure is the weight of the air in the atmosphere pushing down on Earth. Wind is moving air. It begins with air pressure.

Meteorologists measure changes in air pressure to help predict weather.

Low and High Air Pressure

When the Sun heats air, the warm air rises. When air rises, it presses down on Earth less. It creates an area of low pressure. Cold air sinks. Sinking air pushes down more, so it creates an area of high pressure.

The Sun does not heat Earth in all the same places at the same time. Areas of both high and low pressure are everywhere.

Air usually flows from areas of high pressure to low pressure. Air moving between areas of pressure is wind. The greater the difference between the high and low pressure areas, the stronger the wind.

The highest non-tornado wind speed ever recorded was 253 mph (407 km/h).

Energy in Motion

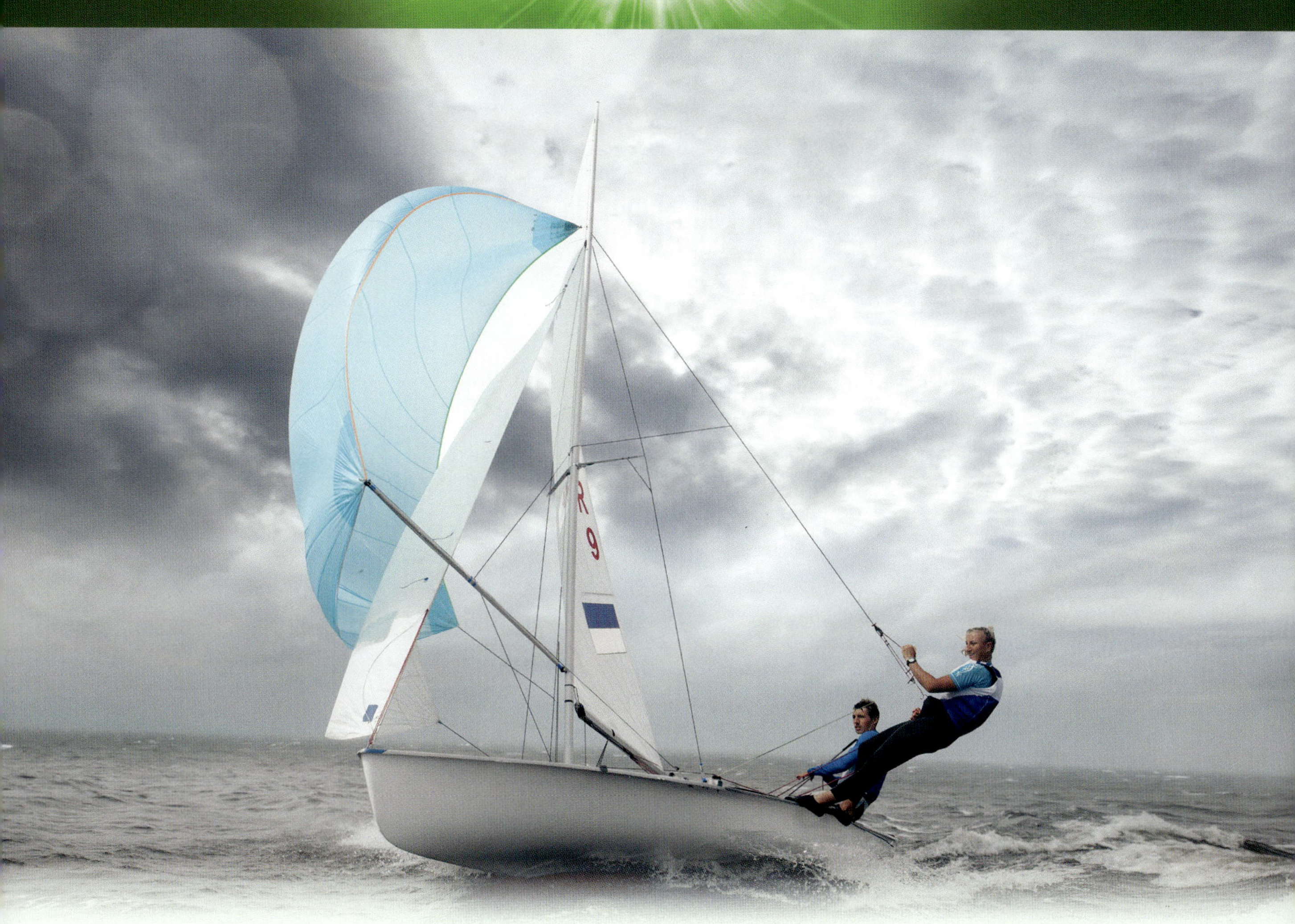

Energy in Motion

Energy in motion is called **kinetic** energy. Since wind is air in motion, wind has kinetic energy. The faster and stronger the wind, the more energy it has. We cannot pull energy out of the wind, but we can use it in a different way.

Chapter 3: Capturing Wind Energy

A sailboat moves by using the wind's kinetic energy. The force of the wind against the sails pushes the boat. Ancient Egyptians may have been the first to build boats with sails nearly 5,000 years ago. Boats used wind power until engines were invented. Sailboats still do.

Windmills

A windmill is a machine that uses wind to spin sails. It changes the wind's kinetic energy into **rotational** energy. Windmills were first used in Iran thousands of years ago. They made pumping water or grinding grain faster and easier.

The Netherlands built many windmills. It once had more than 10,000.

Many windmills have four sails. The sails are tilted a bit to catch the wind more easily. They are attached to rods and wheels inside the windmill. The spinning sails turn the rods and wheels. The wheels grind grain or pump water.

Chapter 4: Changing Wind to Power

In a modern wind turbine, the blades are almost 200 feet (61 m) long. They are curved like an airplane's wings. Wind travels faster over a curve.

How do we use wind to make electricity? Today, we use wind **turbines**. They have blades instead of a windmill's sails. A computer tracks the wind and shifts the blades. Moving the blades toward the wind helps them catch its full force.

Other countries are also planning to build taller wind turbines. Both Scotland and China want to build wind turbines around 850 feet (259 m) tall.

Winds blow faster higher up, so wind turbines are tall. Many are around 295 feet (90 m) tall. That's about as high as the Statue of Liberty. Some are taller. Denmark plans to build a wind turbine that will be more than 900 feet (274 m) tall.

Making Electricity

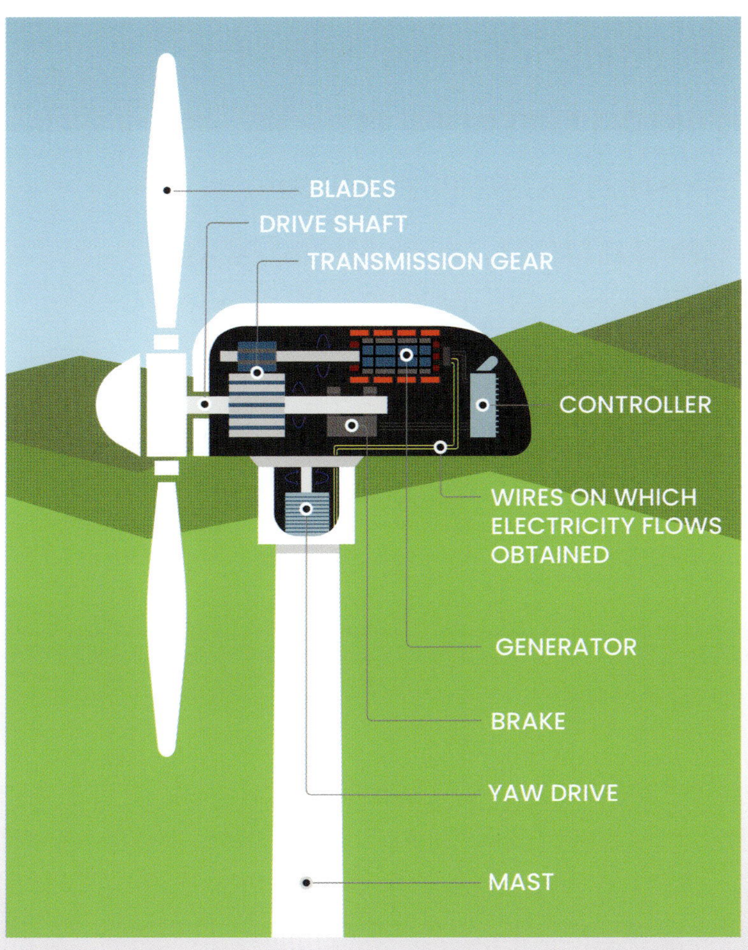

A wind turbine's blades connect to a rod called a drive shaft. The drive shaft connects to a generator. As wind flows over the blades, they spin and turn the drive shaft. Then the drive shaft turns the generator. The generator produces electricity.

A generator is a machine that turns motion into electricity.

Powering a City

Electricity in a power grid may come from both nonrenewable and alternative energy sources.

More than half of the world's countries make some electricity from wind power.

The electricity generated by wind turbines travels through power lines to a **substation**. The substation changes the electricity into a form that can be sent to a **power grid**. All sources of electricity feed into the same power grids.

Smaller substations carry the electricity to towns and cities. Power lines above or below the ground connect them. Electricity flows from the substation into homes, businesses, streetlights, and more.

Chapter 5: Wind Farms

China produces the most wind power in the world. The United States is second, and Germany is third. But China is so large that half of its electricity still comes from nonrenewable energy sources.

A wind farm is an area of land with many wind turbines. Gansu Wind Farm in China is the world's largest. It has 7,000 wind turbines. California's Alta Wind Energy Center is the biggest in the United States. It has 600 wind turbines and powers more than 200,000 homes.

The tips of wind turbine blades sometimes spin at 120 mph (193 km/h).

Offshore Wind Farms

Some wind farms are built in the water near coasts to catch ocean winds. The Hornsea 1 is off England's eastern coast and has 174 wind turbines. It powers one million homes in the United Kingdom. The United Kingdom has the most offshore wind farms in the world.

China has the second-highest number of offshore wind farms. The United States has one offshore wind farm but plans to build more.

Chapter 6: Challenges of Wind Farms

Wind Needed

Wind turbines can only make electricity from wind energy. On days with little or no wind, no electricity is produced. If an area suddenly needs more energy, such as on a very cold day when people use a lot of heat, there is no way to turn up the wind to generate more electricity.

If the wind is too strong, the turbines shut down to keep them from breaking.

Not all places have enough wind for wind farms. Areas with lots of wind can be far from where people live. New power lines and substations must be built to bring electricity from remote wind farms to towns and cities. Building this new equipment requires spending more money.

Cost to Build

Home wind turbines are much smaller than those on wind farms. They help homes in windy areas make their own electricity.

One large wind turbine may cost between 2 million and 4 million dollars. China spent 15 billion dollars to build Gansu Wind Farm. California's Alta Wind Energy Center cost around 2.8 billion dollars. Wind turbines made for home use cost from 15,000 dollars to 75,000 dollars.

A single blade on some wind turbines weighs 27,000 pounds (12,274 kg).

Other Problems

Wind turbine generators hum. The spinning blades make a whooshing sound. Some people feel wind farms are too noisy to build near homes. Others worry that wind turbines may harm wildlife. Birds and bats have been killed by flying into the blades.

Chapter 7: The Future of Wind Power

Wind costs nothing. It will never run out. Wind power is also a clean source of energy. One wind turbine produces enough electricity in 94 minutes to power a home in the United States for one month.

The use of wind power is growing. It is the second most widely used renewable energy source in the world today. However, it still makes less than 10 percent of the world's electricity. Will wind power be used more in the future?

Glossary

alternative (ahl-TUR-nuh-tive): Something that may be chosen instead of something else

carbon dioxide (CAR-bun dye-OX-ide): A gas that is produced when people or animals breathe out or when certain fuels are burned

climate (KLEYE-muht): The usual weather conditions of a particular place

kinetic (kuh-NEH-tick): Something caused by or relating to motion

meteorologist (mee-tee-uh-ROL-uh-jist): A type of scientist who studies Earth's atmosphere to understand and predict the weather

power grid (PAU-ur GRID): A connected system for delivering electrical power from power plants to homes and businesses

rotational (row-TAY-shuh-nuhl): The act of turning around a center

substation (SUHB-stay-shn): Equipment that makes electricity usable for people

turbine (TUR-bin or TUR-bahyn): A machine that has a part with blades that are caused to spin by pressure from water, steam, or air

Index

Comprehension Questions

1. What makes wind?
   a. Air is pushed by the heavy atmosphere
   b. Air moves between areas of high and low pressure
   c. Air is stirred up by the Sun
2. What happens when wind blows against a wind turbine?
   a. The turbine soaks up the wind
   b. The turbine reflects the wind
   c. The turbine spins
3. What is one of the challenges of wind power?
   a. Wind turbines are noisy
   b. Wind turbines break easily
   c. Wind power will run out
4. True or False: Nonrenewable energy sources can be replaced.
5. True or False: Some wind farms are built in water near coasts.

Comprehension questions answer key: 1. b 2. c 3. a 4. False 5. True

About the Author

Tracy Vonder Brink loves true stories and facts. She has written more than 20 books for kids and is a contributing editor for three children's science magazines. Tracy lives in Cincinnati, Ohio, with her husband, two daughters, and two rescue dogs.

Written by: Tracy Vonder Brink
Designed by: Jennifer Bowers
Series Development: James Earley
Proofreader: Melissa Boyce
Educational Consultant: Marie Lemke M.Ed.
Print Coordinator: Katherine Berti

Photographs: cover ©2010 WDG Photo/Shutterstock, ©R2D2/Shutterstock; p.4 ©2021 Lin Xiu Xiu/Shutterstock; p.5 ©2015 Africa Studio/Shutterstock; p.6 ©2020 Natalia Leinonen/Shutterstock; p.7 ©2016 Tatjana Baibakova/ Shutterstock; p8. ©2020 Sunshine Seeds/Shutterstock; p.9 ©2009 Mark Smith/ Shutterstock; p.10 ©2016 Evannovostro/Shutterstock; p.11 ©2020 robuart/ Shutterstock; p.12 ©2012 Peter Wollinga/Shutterstock; p.13 ©2019 Artur Didyk/Shutterstock; p.14 ©2020 Giovanni Rinaldi/Shutterstock; p.15 ©2010 Pavel_Markevych/Shutterstock; p.16 ©2018 K.Sorokin/Shutterstock; p.17 ©2016 Massimo Cavallo/Shutterstock; p.18 ©2016 Oleg Lopatkin/Shutterstock; p.19 ©TatyanaTVK/Shutterstock; p.20-21 ©2017 Soonthorn Wongsaita/Shutterstock; p.22 ©2019 Matyas Rehak/Shutterstock; p.23 ©2015 Nuttawut Uttamaharad/ Shutterstock; p.24 ©2016 Stock2468/Shutterstock; p.25 ©2021 Margus Vilbas Photography/Shutterstock; p.26 ©2019 Ingo Bartussek/Shutterstock; p.27 ©2019 Anda Mikelsone/Shutterstock; p.28-29 ©2017 John-Kelly/Shutterstock

Library and Archives Canada Cataloguing in Publication

Available at the Library and Archives Canada

Library of Congress Cataloging-in-Publication Data

Available at the Library of Congress

Crabtree Publishing Company

www.crabtreebooks.com 1-800-387-7650

Published in the United States
Crabtree Publishing
347 Fifth Avenue
Suite 1402-145
New York, NY, 10016

Published in Canada
Crabtree Publishing
616 Welland Ave.
St. Catharines, ON
L2M 5V6

Printed in the U.S.A./072022/CG20220201